Stories and rhymes in this book

Published by Ladybird Books Ltd
27 Wrights Lane London W8 5TZ
A Penguin Company

Produced for Ladybird Books Ltd by Nicola Baxter and Amanda Hawkes

The Lazy Lions

by Joan Stimson

illustrated by Valeria Petrone

Ladybird

WE'RE THE LAZY LIONS!

We're called
the Lazy Lions,
But WE don't
think we're slow.
And when you get
to know us,
You'll find we're
fun to know.

We may not be high-fliers.
We may not rush around.
But all our friends
will tell you,
We're GRRREAT
to have around!

DARREN'S PARTY

The Lazy Lions had overslept...

even though it was Darren's birthday...

and they'd planned a party.

"Happy Birthday, Darren!" yawned Dad at last. "Here's your present."

"Happy Birthday, Darren!" yawned Lofty the Lodger. "I hope you like this."

Dad and Lofty peered eagerly at the instructions on Darren's construction kit.

Darren peered eagerly at his new watch.

"It's exactly ten minutes until my party," he announced.

Dad and Lofty slid down the bannisters...

and into the kitchen.

"There are sandwiches to make," they gulped.

"And a cake to ice."

"And balloons to blow up," Darren reminded them. "So let's hope my friends all arrive late."

But...
DING, DONG!
DING, DONG!

"Oh dear," said Dad. And he opened the door.

"Oh dear," said Davina. "I didn't know it was a PYJAMA party!" And she ran off to tell the others.

By the time Darren's friends turned up in THEIR pyjamas...

the Lazy Lions were out of breath.

But the party was just...

BRILLIANT!

FAST FOOD

Baked beans
from the tin,

A pizza at
the door,

A chocolate bar with toffee in...

Who could ask for more?

BABYSITTING BECKY

The Lazy Lions were running out of ideas.

They'd agreed to look after their neighbour's baby...

and Becky took a lot of entertaining.

"How about a *little* nap?" said Dad.

But as soon as Becky heard "NAP..." she started bawling.

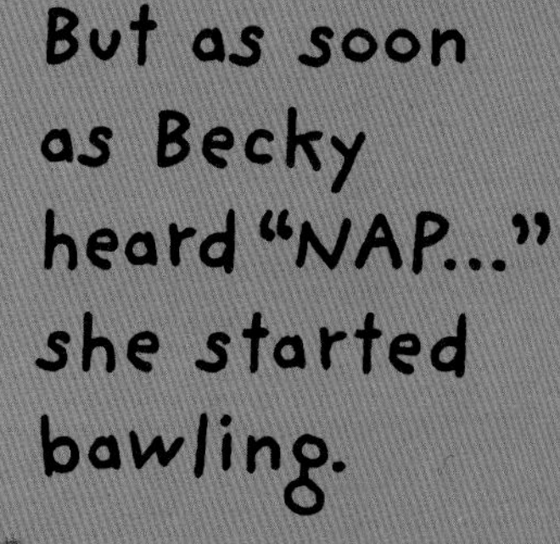

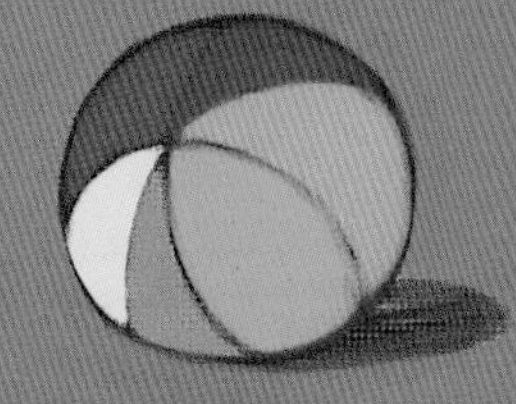

"What about a little lie-down?" said Lofty.

But as soon as Becky heard "LIE-DOWN..." she started yelling.

So the Lazy Lions pulled funny faces to cheer Becky up...

and Becky joined in.

"What about a little snooze?" said Darren.

But as soon as Becky heard "SNOOZE..." she started shrieking.

So the Lazy Lions said, "Let's play hide and seek."

It took a long time for Becky to find Dad, Darren and Lofty...

and when she did, they were all making a strange noise.

Becky was determined to make the strange noise, too.

And just as her mum came to collect her...

she did!

HOT TIPS FOR COOL SWIMMERS

There's no need to dive,
Just FLOP in the pool.
You'll find that the water
Is lovely and cool.

Flip yourself over
And float on your back,
Then swoosh up and down,
You'll SOON get the knack.

THE RACE

It was the day of the Lions' Fun Run. And Lofty had a confession to make.

"I've put your names down for the Father and Son Race," he told Darren and Dad.

"Is there a prize for coming last?" asked Darren, hopefully.

Dad blew the dust off their trainers...

and they loped along to the track.

But they were WORRIED when they saw...

the other lions.

At last it was time for the race to begin. The other lions jogged eagerly on the spot.

But then the organizer made them stand still...

so she could tie the dads' left legs to their sons' right ones.

"Oh, no," groaned the sporty lions.

"It's a THREE-LEGGED race!"

But Darren and Dad beamed.
"This is easy," they said.

And they strolled slowly but surely past the finishing post – first!

YUMMY!

You've got cherries in your whiskers...
And ice cream in your fur!

You must have had the kind of treat...
That makes a lion PURR!

BIG EFFORT DAY

The Lazy Lions peered at the big cross on their calendar.

"It can't be a whole year since our last tidy-up," they told each other.

And when they realized it WAS time for a Big Effort Day...

they flopped into their deckchairs to recover.

At last Lofty began to make a list.

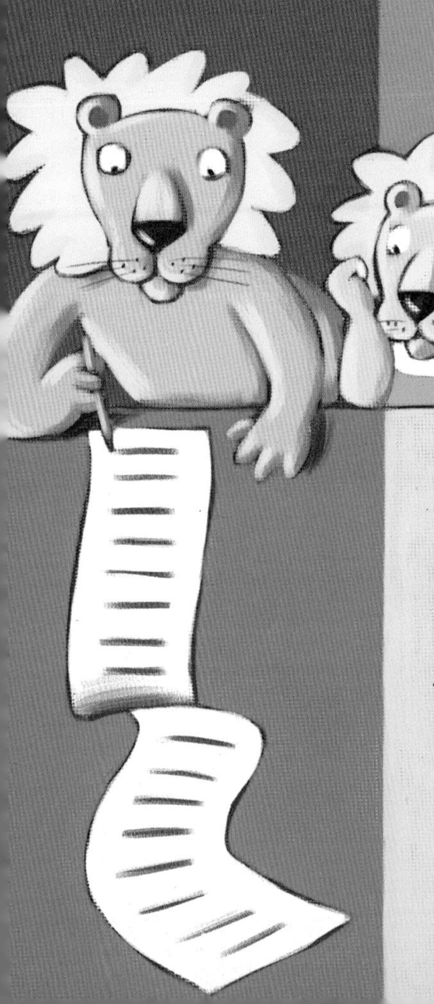

Dad and Darren were already feeling depressed.

But then...
"Cooee!
Cooee!"

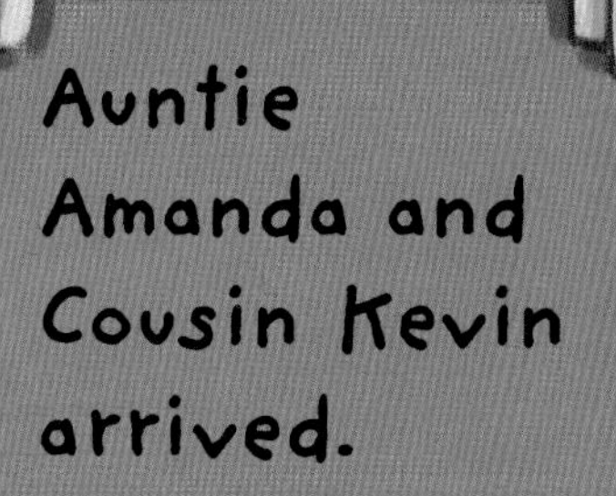

Auntie Amanda and Cousin Kevin arrived.

"Kevin has joined the Safari Cubs," announced Auntie proudly.

"He has to collect as much as he possibly can for the Recycling Centre."

WHOOOOOSH! Dad, Darren and Lofty leapt to their feet.

ZOOOM!
They zipped
round the
house...
pointing...
and panting.

Kevin was delighted with his record-breaking rubbish collection.

And the Lazy Lions had to admit...

"Big Effort Day wasn't so bad after all!"

LION EXPRESS

Whoops-a-Lazy Lion,
Wobbling on your way,
Whoops-a-Lazy Lion,
There's something I must say,

Whoops-a-Lazy Lion,
As you go whizzing past,
Whoops-a-Lazy Lion,
You're going REALLY FAST!